I0623604

After Dawn Breaks

Nat T. Hill

Published by TaiLorMade Books

Chapter 1

"She only has a few months, maybe weeks to live. She's not eating or retaining any fluids. She's lost five pounds in the last week. All of her vital body parts will start shutting down. There's nothing we can do." Dr. Morrow explained.

"No!" Valerie screamed. "This can't be. This is my baby! She's all I have!"

"I'm sorry Ms. Johnson," Dr. Morrow said, slowly exiting the room.

Joe Johnson grabbed his wife as she hysterically screamed in his arms. He felt so helpless and couldn't console her because of his overwhelming sorrow.

"Valerie listen, I need you to be brave for me, okay?"

"Joe, what are we going to do?" Ms. Johnson cried out.

"Do you remember my old friend, Dr. Welch, from college? I haven't spoken to him in a while, but at least we can get a second opinion."

"Wait...isn't that the guy who does-"

"Yes," Joe quickly interrupted, "but he's the only option we have."

Val hadn't seen Dr. Welch in years and from what she knew, he was no longer able to perform practices in the United States. He and Joe were good friends back in college until Dr. Welch accused Joe of stealing one of his scientific projects for a $150,000 grant that Joe had received. Joe claimed that he came up with the idea and Dr. Welch simply funded the materials needed for the project. Even though Joe gave Dr. Welch $10,000 of the winnings, which was four times more than what Dr. Welch had contributed, Dr. Welch was salty, and the friendship became an effortless hi and bye.

It was six in the evening and it was a two-hour drive back home from Dawn Lynn's specialist. Mrs. Johnson stared blankly out of the car window as their four-year-old, Dawn Lynn rested in the back seat of their Audi SUV. Although they had been battling with their daughter's sickness for the past year or so, what Dr. Morrow said was the last thing she wanted to hear. How could someone who was supposed to be a professional and had studied in his field for many years say that it was hopeless? Had he even tried to find an alternative?

Dawn Lynn was diagnosed with a rare disease that attacks all the major organs in the body. It was a genetic disorder that is commonly found in elderly people, but somehow the gene formed early inside of Dawn Lynn. Joe and Valerie were unaware it existed in either sides of their families. She didn't know how she would be able to bare life without her baby girl. She had actually made up in her mind that she wouldn't.

Valerie had decided that if Dawn Lynn died, she would also take her life as well. Valerie was afraid of guns and didn't want to suffer during her predetermined death. She decided that overdosing on sleeping pills would be the best solution. She knew Joe would probably be devastated losing both her and their daughter, but she'd rather him be happy with someone else than to live with her in misery. Besides, it wasn't like they were doing well in their marriage anyway.

After arriving home, Dawn Lynn was peacefully sleeping from the treatments they gave her earlier at the doctor's office. Joe put her in her royal king-sized princess bed they had bought her for her second birthday and proceeded to call Dr. Welch as planned. Dawn Lynn was their only child of their six-year marriage and was the glue that kept them together.

Joe was a very successful business owner of two-night clubs and a cleaning business. Joe had been accused of having several affairs with his female subordinates but denied them all. Even though Val suspected infidelity from his persistent nights of coming in late and sometimes even in the early mornings, he would always blame it on trouble at one of the clubs. Valerie became a stay-at-home mom after Dawn Lynn became sick, so she really didn't have the time to investigate. All of her focus and energy went to Dawn Lynn. Before then, Valerie owned a catering company that she sold for a quarter of a million dollars.

"I called Dr. Welch and talked about setting up a meeting for this Friday. I told him I would talk it over with you and would call him back to confirm it." He explained to Valerie.

"I don't know if I'm ready to take the risk, Joe. I need Dr. Welch to promise me that our daughter will get better if we bring her to him."

"He said that he couldn't guarantee anything but was willing to do everything that he possibly could," explained Mr. Johnson, sitting down on the couch next to his weary wife. "He's no different from any other human being. Even with a normal surgery with licensed physicians they tell you that it's a practice. That's why you sign all those papers, releasing them of any probable death."

"Just stop using that word. Please!"

"I'm sorry, Val. I know this is hard for you. It's hard for me as well. You know I am willing to do what I can to fix this. I don't know any other solution. What else can we do?"

Valerie sat and thought about what her husband was saying. The fact of the matter was she was going to be weary of anything that was presented no matter who presented it. Joe made a good point. What other option did they have? She wondered was Dr. Welch even in the right headspace to do this.

"Did he seem as if he still has a grudge?" she asked.

"Well, no. He was kind of surprised to hear from me, but when I told him the severity of our baby's condition, he seemed eager to help."

"Does he still practice in his lab behind his home?"

"I'm assuming so since the board dismissed him."

"How long was that ago?"

"I'm guessing about five years."

"I really don't know about this, Joe. What exactly does he want to do? Will it be surgery, treatments, or some type of experimental medicines?"

"Listen, I know we've heard some strange things about a few of his experiments going wrong, but he has had a lot of successes with healing people. There is no other choice that we have at this point."

"The Wilsons said that their son, Tommy loss his speech after going to Dr. Welch and the child before that went blind," Valerie complained.

"The Wilson's son didn't have what Dawn has, and we can't confirm that any of those instances were Dr. Welch's doing. What we both can say is that those children are still alive, so think about what we're comparing, the loss of our daughter's voice or sight, or the loss of our daughter."

Even though Joe made a valid argument, it still didn't put Valerie's mind at ease about Dr. Welch's practices. Of course, she wanted her baby to live without a question, but she didn't want her daughter to have to suffer through life either. What if this experiment caused Dawn Lynn even more pain from unexpected side effects? From the way Joe talked, her daughter would be used as a guinea pig for something Dr. Welch had thrown together in a few containers. Worst of all, what if Dr. Welch's treatment failed and caused instantaneous death?

Chapter 2

A few hours later Joe and Valerie were still sitting on the sofa discussing their options. Everything felt like a lose-lose situation and the only logical answer to Joe was calling Dr. Welch. He was getting frustrated as Valerie continued to question his practices.

"Look, Val. We've been discussing this for hours now and I'm tired. You continue to quiz me about the uncertainty when nothing is certain. Meanwhile, our daughter is still lying in the bed suffering."

"I realize that, Joe, but have you considered what happens if he fails?"

"Have you realized the severity of the condition that our daughter is already in? Every other doctor she's had has failed."

They were suddenly interrupted by the buzzing of Joe's phone. He looked down at the call and didn't bother to answer it. Valerie was tired of his secrecy. It was enough that she was dealing with Dawn's sickness, but the lies and late-night meetings at the club took her overboard.

"Aren't you going to answer that," she insisted.

"It's just the club. I told them I would be down there an hour ago, but instead I'm here arguing with you about a simple solution."

"Are you implying that the health of our daughter is less important than your whorish club?"

"This is a subject that is off limits. I am the one who pays the bills around here and all the medical expenses for Dawn, so what you feel about my job is irrelevant."

"I just recently sold that catering business to cater to our sick daughter you asshole. It's not like you've been doing this forever. It's not like you were going to give up your career to wait on her hand and foot. You'd rather please those tramps at the club."

"I don't have time for your nonsense. I'll be back when I get back so don't wait up," he said, getting up from the sofa.

She threw the remote control across the room, barely missing his head. He turned around and walked over towards her as if he was about to react. Before he could reach her, they both heard a soft patter on the floor.

"Mommy, I can't sleep, and my tummy hurt," said Dawn, hobbling into the living room and resting on her mother's lap. Her head was hot, and she was sweating from her reaction to the treatment the doctor gave her earlier. It took everything in Valerie not to cry, but she knew she had to be strong for her daughter. As she held her sick child in her arms, Valerie knew that creating hypothetical side effects in her mind didn't matter. She was willing to do any and everything to keep her child alive. She gave Joe "a thumb up" to call Dr. Welch as she rocked her child in her arms. As soon as he made the appointment, he walked out without telling her or Dawn Lynn goodbye.

By the middle of the week, Dawn Lynn continued to lose weight, nearly becoming skin and bones. Her voice became muffled and she could no longer walk on her own. Around noon as Val rocked her sickly child in her arms, she decided that she couldn't wait a minute longer. She was going to see Dr Welch two days before her scheduled appointment. She gathered up some clothes, toys, and a few other personal items since she wasn't sure how long they would have to stay. Joe wasn't home as usual, so she got the directions he had stuck on the refrigerator and headed out to find Dr. Welch.

After missing a few left and right turns, she finally found Dr. Welch's home about an hour later. His driveway stemmed from a long dirt road and was isolated from the neighbor's view. His house was made like an old castle and Val could see the top and a side portion of the ominous barn house behind it where Dr. Welch probably did his lab work. Leaving the car running under his giant outdoor foyer, she ran to his front door and frantically rang the doorbell.

"Dr. Welch, please help me she yelled," starting to feel her adrenaline rush.

A tall, fair-skinned man with grayish eyes in a lab coat came to the door.

"Hello, ma'am, can I help you?"

"Hi, is Dr. Welch home."

"He's working in the lab. I'm his assistant, Greg Mills."

"Pleasure to meet you Greg, listen, I really need to see Dr. Welch immediately."

"I'm sorry ma'am, I can not disturb him while he's working."

"No, but you don't understand-"

"I'm sorry ma'am, but you have to leave," he demanded, shutting the door.

"This is an emergency!" she yelled after him.

Val was in tears as she banged on the door in hopes that he would turn around and come back. He continued to walk as if she didn't exist. She needed to see Dr. Welch immediately, but she wasn't sure how she could get to him. She quickly remembered that the assistant said that Dr. Welch was over in the lab working. She got in her car and pretended to leave the premises, but instead, she drove around in a circle and hid her car at the back of Dr. Welch's barn. She picked up Dawn Lynn from the back seat, wrapped her legs around her waist, and carried her to a glass door she found on the side of the barn. She couldn't see anyone from her view, so she banged on the glass as hard as she could with her only free fist.

"Dr. Welch, help. I'm here. Dawn Lynn is dying!" Valerie cried.

Greg must have already been on his way to tell Dr. Welch about his visitor because he spotted her. "Hey, ma'am, get away from there!" He screamed, jogging toward her.

Valerie felt hopeless. She was going to lose her daughter.

Chapter 3

"Dr. Welch, help!" Val screamed even louder.

"Ma'am, you and your child cannot be here right now!"

"Look here assistant guy, my baby is dying and you're going to have to kill me before I step foot off this premises without seeing him."

The yelling between the two made Dawn Lynn let out a soft cry in her mother's arms. Val gently squeezed her closer to her chest as Greg put his arms on his head not knowing what to do. As fate would have it, Val saw Dr. Welch walking toward his house from a back entrance.

"Dr. Welch! Dr. Welch!" yelled Val, walking as quickly as she could with a tight hold to Dawn Lynn.

Dr. Welch stopped and put one hand over his forehead as if he was trying to get a better view. Finally catching up to him, Val was too out of breath to explain.

"Dr. Welch, I am so sorry. I told her you were working on something urgent and for her to leave the premises." Greg said, following behind the two.

"You're kidding me, right?" Dr. Welch asked him, turning his attention back to Val and Dawn.

"No sir, I'm not. Do you want me to call the authorities?"

"You made this weary woman chase me around this huge barn with her pale child in her arms?"

"Dr. Welch I didn't know you wanted-"

"Excuse me ma'am, if I may?" He asked, interrupting Greg while reaching out his hands to carry Dawn Lynn sideways in both his arms.

"Dr. Welch, I didn't know the child was sick." Greg said, trying again to explain.

"Follow me this way, Miss. Oh, uh...Greg, I think your duties are done for today. I'll call you if I need any further assistance."

"But what about the project, sir?"

"Cancel my 3 o'clock and any other appointments I had scheduled. That will be all, Greg."

Greg opened the front door as Dr. Welch walked in with Dawn Lynn and Val behind him. He seemed very disappointed as he obediently left the lab. Dr. Welch put Dawn Lynn on a bed that resembled an operating table and checked her heartbeat. He then checked her temperature and lifted up the railing for her safety.

"I'm glad you went ahead and brought her in Mrs. Johnson. Her heartbeat is irregular, and her temperature is extremely high. I have to get started right away."

"I didn't think you would remember who I was after all these years."

"Some faces you never forget. Now, your husband was explaining that the specialist said that there was nothing he could do about her rare condition, correct?"

"Yes, sir."

"I've been doing some additional research since Joe's phone call and to be perfectly honest, there's not anything "scientific" that I could do to help your daughter's situation."

"You say that as if there is another alternative."

"Well, it's quite complex. I've been working on an anti-aging serum that is formulated to counteract a variety of medical conditions found in elderly patients. We haven't had the appropriate resources to thoroughly test the serum, so I'm skeptical about using your daughter as our first youth patient, especially since she's obviously underdeveloped compared to an adult."

"Is there anyway you could modify the serum? Perhaps you could use an eighth of what you would normally use for an elderly patient."

"Uh...the suggestion sounds great, but the potency would not change. Her organs are overdeveloped, but her body isn't. This means one of two things could happen. Her body could accept the serum and reverse the aging of her vital organs, which would eventually align together as she gets older."

"So, she would be a normal child?"

"Absolutely, everything will develop as if the aging never existed. However, a worse case scenario is that her small body could counteract the serum, speeding up the aging process causing death within a few days or even hours."

Valerie took a step outside knowing she was facing the hardest decision of her life. She was already losing her baby girl but telling him to use the serum and it didn't work meant that she speeded up this process to end Dawn Lynn's life. She considered calling Joe, but knowing him, he would tell her to wait until the weekend and time was of the essence. She looked up toward the clouds, closed her eyes, and said a prayer before having to give Dr. Welch her decision.

"Dr. Welch, I'm in an extremely vulnerable position," Valerie began, walking back into the barn, gently grabbing one of his hands with both of her hands with a firm grip.

"Without Dawn Lynn, I have nothing. My marriage has been failing for years, my company is gone, and my soul is dying. I need her and will not live without her."

"I will do all that I can," he said, putting his other hand on top of hers while giving her a reassuring shake.

"Thank you," she said, giving him a nod of gratitude before walking over to Dawn Lynn.

Her precious baby looked helpless curled up under the blue blanket that Dr. Welch had put over her. Valerie knew she was not only making the hardest decision of her life, but Dawn Lynn's life as well.

She leaned down and gave her daughter a soft kiss on the forehead. She held her tiny hand and whispered how much she loved her. Trying not to be insensitive, Dr. Welch gently touched her elbow and told Valerie that he must get started right away. She turned around as she instinctively buried her face in his lab coat. He gave her a comfort hug with one arm and pulled his cell phone from his pocket with the other.

He called his butler to make sure the guest room was in proper order and for him to come down and escort Valerie in his home. She refused to leave Dawn Lynn's side. Dr. Welch again explained that the procedure was timely and extremely complicated. He tried to give her a visual of how meticulous he had to be when it came to injecting the serum near specific parts of her tiny organs.

He also informed her that it would take at least ten to twelve hours before the process was fully completed and an additional eight hours before she could visit. He let her know that his assistant nurse, Carol would be arriving soon and would also be there around the clock to help with Dawn Lynn.

After finally complying with Dr. Welch's wishes, Valerie tried to settle into the guest room as best she could. Although she felt better knowing that her baby would have a mother-like figure with her throughout the procedure, she knew her anxiety would reach new heights. She couldn't help but to imagine her child crying out for her at some point. Would the nurse comfort her baby or just monitor her and allow the continuous cries? Valerie knew she had to do something else to distract herself from the negative possibilities flooding her mind. She decided that it would be a good time to fill Joe in on everything that had transpired.

"Hello, Joe Johnson's assistant Donna speaking."

"Why are you answering Joe's personal cell phone?"

"Because I'm his assistant, duh. Who is this?"

"This is his wife, you dimwit. Where is my husband?"

"You have the nerve to call me a dimwit, but you're the one who is unaware of your husband's whereabouts."

"Look, I don't have time to play. Put my husband on the phone now."

"Mr. Johnson isn't available. You can call back and I will allow you to leave a voicemail."

"I am not calling my husband back. You're the assistant so assist with giving him his phone.

"As I stated. Mr. Johnson is busy at the time. Thank you for your call. Have a good night as we plan to do."

Chapter 4

Valerie was outraged as the assistant ended the call. Even though Donna didn't come out and say it, there was some indication that she was more than just an assistant. She couldn't believe the disrespect that she had just encountered. The nerve of this woman to speak to her that way was one thing, but Joe allowing this woman to have full access to his personal cell phone was an entirely different issue alone. It was clear since he didn't respect her that his staff wasn't going to either. Enough was enough. Valerie decided that she and Dawn Lynn were going to be fine on their own.

Unable to get any sleep, Valerie sat on the guest bed wondering what was going on with Dawn Lynn. As much as she wanted to go back down to Dr. Welch's lab, she knew she was given specific instructions not to disturb him. Starting to feel dehydrated, she needed something to drink.

Vaguely remembering where the kitchen was, Valerie quietly left her room and crept down the hall. She felt as if she was walking through a hunted house in a story book. After making a left turn, she saw a room with the door slightly opened further up the hall. From what she knew, Dr Welch wasn't married or didn't have kids living with him. Overcome by curiosity she crept slowly toward the door.

She put her ear towards the door to see if she could hear someone in the room. Dead silence. Cautiously pushing it open, there was a small lamp that hovered over a tall table stand. She knew she was eavesdropping, but the mystery in Dr. Welch kept her intrigued. Besides, he literally held her daughter's life in his hands. It was her right to find out everything she could about him. She took another look back as she edged over to the table. There were several sketches similar to Dr. Welch's home. To the right, she saw a blueprint labeled as "lower dungeon" with a red **X** beside it. Chill bumps rolled up her arms as a shiver of fear swept through her body. *What was Dr. Welch planning to do? What did he keep in this lower dungeon*? Sticking out underneath the blueprint, she saw several negative transactions on a bank statement. It appeared as if he was also in debt. Just as she went to grab it, she felt a touch from behind.

"Ahhh!" She sharply squealed.

"Can I help you, madam?" The butler asked, quickly jerking his arm back from her sudden fright.

"Oh God, you scared me," she said.

She noticed the intent stare he was giving her as he waited for a response. The truth was she didn't have one. It was more than obvious she was snooping, so she had to explain what she could be snooping for.

"I'm sorry. I didn't mean to be intrusive. I'm very nervous and worried about my daughter, so I wanted to see if I could find something to explain the procedure."

It was a damn good explanation. It was so good that he seemed to loosen up as he gave her a half smile.

"Come madam," he insisted, offering his arm, "Your daughter is in great hands."

He shut off the lamp with a quick pull of the beaded chain and quietly closed the door. He escorted Valerie to the kitchen and made her some warm tea. He began to discuss how he first met Dr. Welch and how he was marveled by his practices. He told her he had a granddaughter that was told would never see again. With the help of Dr. Welch, his granddaughter did what doctors said was impossible and gained her eyesight. Although she died years later from other complications, Dr. Welch gave her an experience that literally opened her eyes to a whole new world. And for that, he promised to work for Dr. Welch indefinitely without pay.

Hearing his story not only brought tears to Valerie's eyes, but it also gave her a different perspective. She was that much more optimistic about her own daughter's recovery. A feeling of gratitude and warmth overcame as she returned to her room. For the first time in months, she had a peaceful slumber.

Sun rays kissed Valerie's cheeks as they beamed through the giant window of the castle like fortress. She woke up slightly confused about her surroundings. After a few seconds of remembering where she was and why she was there, she ran to the guest bathroom, splashed water on her face, and put on her shoes. She was already fully dressed as she rushed out of the door to go find her baby. Once she got down to the lab, she pulled the door, but it was locked. She tried to peek in through a window, but all she could see was metal shelving. Panic quickly overcame her as she ran back to the house.

"Your daughter is in the kitchen, madam," the butler said as he met her at the front door noticing her anxiety.

She quickly walked through the halls toward the kitchen. Her heart suddenly became elated when she saw her baby girl dancing at the table with toast in her hand.

"Good morning, mommy!" Dawn Lynn squealed.

Valerie dropped to her knees and covered her mouth as tears formed in her eyes. She had been waiting for this moment for what seemed like an eternity. She had her baby back.

"What's wrong, mommy?" Dawn Lynn asked, rushing over to embrace her.

"Oh nothing, Sweetie! Mommy is just really happy."

"Oh okay, mommy. Look what I can do." She said, running over to the table and lifting it from underneath with her arms. Without a wobble, she giddily laughed as she perfectly balanced the table and all its contents.

"Dawn Lynn, no!" Valerie quickly screamed, now noticing the child was still giggling. "What on earth?"

"I know this is a bit much to take in," Dr. Welch began, "I came to your room to discuss some things with you earlier, but you were sound asleep. Dawn Lynn, dear, could you sit and finish your breakfast while I speak with mommy in the hall?"

Dawn Lynn nodded, put down the table, and sat back down to eat.

"Dawn Lynn's recovery is nothing short of a miracle. I was under the impression that her small body would need time to adjust to the serum, but it almost felt like the serum was formulated perfectly for her."

"This is...this is... I don't know what this is! I'm looking at my happy, jovial baby girl lift a freakin' table over her head! How do you react to that after seeing her literally not being able to walk a few hours ago?"

"I know things seem overwhelming and I can't begin to think that I know how you feel. I'm just honored that you trusted me with your daughter's life and that I could help restore what was there."

"There's no way I could ever repay you for what you've done. Not only have you revived my spirit, but you've given me a reason to live again. I know it may not be up to your standards, but if you will allow me, I can set up monthly payments and give you a lump sum when my divorce settlement is final."

"Oh my gosh, Val. Are you really going through a divorce at a time like this?"

Valerie leaned back against wall and put her head down. Her reality quickly set back in when she reminded herself that her marriage was done. Valerie felt embarrassed as tears slowly began to roll down her face.

"Look Val," he said, gently grabbing her hand to show his concern. "I came into this not knowing what to expect. This experience is new for us both. Had things not worked out as well as they did, I wouldn't have dare asked for compensation. So now that she's safe and back to being a bubbling little girl, it wouldn't make sense to charge you now."

"That's nice of you Dr. Welch but I couldn't..."

"I insist."

"Thank you, Dr. Welch. If there's anything I can do for you at all, please don't hesitate to ask. Even if it means baking you a cake once a week," she giggled and smiled, "just let me know."

"That sounds lovely, but I'm quite alright. I do need a small favor however."

"Anything doctor. You name it."

"I would like to monitor and take a sample of Dawn Lynn's blood at least once a year. I want to make sure the serum continues to be effective. And of course, we want to be aware of any possible negative side effects.

"Yes Dr. Welch. I can and will agree to those conditions."

She pulled Dr. Welch close and embraced him with a long, tight hug. Without thinking, she instantaneously placed a heartfelt kiss smack on the doctor's lips. Although she was acting out of pure gratitude and excitement, there was also unknowingly a tad bit of personal attraction from both ends.

Chapter 5

The next day, Dr. Welch sat in his laboratory studying the results of Dawn Lynn's miraculous recovery. He knew this discovery would be just what he needed to get his license back. Valerie had agreed to come back the following weekend for a basic check up to see how the serum was continuing to react in Dawn Lynn's body. He realized that this would still need to be an ongoing study before he was able to submit his findings to the Centers for Disease Control and Prevention, but he was willing to do whatever it took.

It was Dr. Welch's belief that Dawn Lynn would get stronger as she aged. Under the microscope, it appeared as if certain cells in Dawn Lynn's body were increasing in size at an extremely slow rate. This led him to the conclusion by the time she was twenty-five; it was feasible that she may be able to throw a full-sized SUV with her bare hands. This much strength would have to involve some type of negative cell carrier, which is why he needed her to be a continuous study, perhaps once a month opposed to the annual offer he had discussed with Valerie.

Beyond the study of Dawn Lynn, Dr. Welch found himself still very attracted to Valerie. He'd been attracted to her since him and Joe's college days. Back then, Dr. Welch would send her flowers as her secret admirer, but unknowing to Valerie, Joe would intercept them and write his name on it. After Dr. Welch found out what Joe was doing, he told Valerie who still chose Joe as her mate. Although he didn't hold any grudges against Valerie, he knew then that Joe was a snake. So, it didn't surprise him when Joe had stolen one of his formulas and gained access to the huge grant, which ultimately led to their demise as friends.

All that was many years ago and Dr. Welch had left the past where it belonged. He had married, divorced, and had done it all over again by this time. It was a new day and new opportunity for new things. He was excited about where he was headed with his newly developed serum and even more optimistic when Valerie told him she was divorcing Joe. He surely hoped that something would develop between them.

Not wanting to waste any time, Dr. Welch immediately had begun to run test in his laboratory with mice. Although it was nothing comparable to a human body, he could adjust the injections to see if the mice would exhibit any abnormal strength. This would also help him discover any abnormalities the serum could exhibit. He wrote down measurements and other detailed information as to what he was administering to both male and female mice. He was deeply involved in his experimentation until he was slightly startled by a screeching noise.

"Dr. Welch. I see you finally made it happen. Congratulations," assistant Greg commented, barging his way through the doors while clapping his black leather gloves together.

"I wasn't expecting you until the weekend. For what reason do I deserve this delightful disruption?" Dr. Welch asked, not bothering to turn around.

"Wow. You mean to tell me after all of the work I've put in for you that I'm a mere *delightful disruption*. Do those two words even go together?"

"I'm busy, Greg. See you in a few days."

"I see you're being the usual you. Standoffish and rude."

"Thank you, Greg. See you in a few days."

"No, I think we need to talk now, Dr. Welch," Greg demanded, easing out his gun.

"Look dammit, I am in the middle of something big and I ..."

An aggravated Dr. Welch finally turned around to see Greg pointing the weapon at him with two men standing to his side.

"You little prick," Dr. Welch stated, "What are you doing here with these men?"

"Oh, we came to ask for the serum. If you refuse to give it to us… well then…we'll just take it."

"How could you after all I've done for you?"

"How could I? Are you serious? Do you know how much money this is worth? This serum is going to change mankind. I am up my ass in debt from your minimum wage paying ass and I need that money."

Dr. Welch began to laugh hysterically. "You really are an idiot."

The men looked around not knowing what to do. Dr. Welch's laugh was rather haunting and caused Greg sheer embarrassment. Even the two other men were now giggling in the background.

"And you really are a dead man," Greg said, lifting the gun towards Dr. Welch's chest.

"The serum is gone." Dr. Welch said, still laughing. "You have nothing. You're right where you started. I can't believe you brought these two losers for..."

"SHUT UP!" Greg yelled, letting off a round in Dr. Welch's chest.

The laboratory was so quiet that a feather landing would echo. The men with Greg were shocked. This definitely wasn't a part of the plan as one man turned his face and the other pushed Greg's arm.

"What are you, a moron?" One of the men asked. "Now we'll never get the serum. Doctor K will be pissed and I'm not taking the rap for you again."

"I didn't ask you to, did I? Stop with all this bullshit complaining. It's gotta be here somewhere. It's a long, clear tube with a white, yellow, and blue label."

"How big is it?"

"Its pocket size."

"What color is the top?"

"I don't know. It's red I think."

"Where was the last place you saw it?"

"What are these sixty-one questions about this damn tube? Let's just find it already," Greg demanded.

As a pool of blood began to form around Dr. Welch's body, the gang rummaged through shelves and drawers for the tiny bottle that Greg had described. One of the men noticed a similar bottle in the trash can with empty contents. Once Greg observed it, he cursed and then kicked Dr. Welch's leg.

"Now what?" The guy asked.

Greg smashed his fist on a table and began pacing back and forth. He didn't realize how much hatred he had for Dr. Welch. Dr. Welch was always condescending towards him, even when company came to visit the lab.

"Wait a minute," Greg said. "There was a little sick girl and her mother over here the other day when I had originally planned to get the serum. Perhaps he used it on her."

Greg searched Dr. Welch's pockets, but couldn't find his phone. After giving Dr. Welch an additional kick, they left the lab and headed to the main house.

After hearing them leave, Dr. Welch used his elbow to scoot his body over towards his private drawer where he kept his phone when he worked.

"Hello Dr. Welch," Valerie joyously answered.

"Val...al," he slurred, "listen...you've got... you've got to...get out of town. There coming...for Dawn."

"Dr. Welch! What's going on? Are you okay?"

"They want...they want the serum in her blood."

"I don't understand. I'm calling the police," she said, shaken with fear.

"No... no. It's too...too late for me. Take Dawn and leave town...now."

The phone went silent.

Chapter 6

A few years had passed, and Valerie still remembered that dreadful night. It was headlined all over the news.

Prominent Scientist Found Dead Along with Two Others

The case went cold as the police were unable to apprehend any liable suspects. Valerie remembered how strange Dr. Welch's assistant was acting around that time, but when she saw him in the news crying for help with the investigation, she presumed he was innocent. She couldn't understand how people could be so cruel. She thought how nice Dr. Welch's butler was to her the night she was there and the miracle that Dr. Welch had created for them both. The only consolation in the matter was that the butler could now join his granddaughter on the other side.

Valerie was also disappointed that she didn't get to know Dr. Welch. Besides being forever indebted by his services, she found him handsome and mysterious. She hated the reality of wondering what could have been between them.

What shook Valerie even more was the thought of what could have happened if Dawn Lynn had still been there recovering. These intruders didn't have any human decency, so there was no telling what they would have done to either one of them. Dr. Welch said with his final breath that the killers were after the serum, which had now settled into her daughter's veins. She didn't waste a minute taking heed to Dr. Welch's orders. She had quickly packed their bags, took a few necessary items, and took off without her husband. From that day forth, she had to protect her child by any means.

Valerie felt it was better to home school Dawn Lynn until she was able to gain the full concept of her capabilities. They moved often, and Valerie changed her name from time to time. She had her lawyer deliver the divorce papers to Joe and a few months later she received a large settlement amount from the house sell and other assets in the divorce decree.

*   *   *

It was Dawn Lynn's birthday and she had planned a sweet 16 party with a few associates. She was fully aware of her strength and the responsibilities that came with it. She understood why her mom was so protective and elated when she was allowed to go to a normal school with other kids. They had been in the same city for almost two years, which was a surprise to Dawn Lynn. Her mother agreed to go to the local party store to pick up decorations and partying gifts.

"Come on Dawn Lynn, we don't want the party to start late."

"Coming mom!" Dawn yelled from upstairs in their rented townhouse.

"Mom, I think it would be so cool to add like some earrings to the girls gift bags," she said, walking down while fixing the diamond earrings in her ear that her dad sent.

"Wow, I hadn't seen those. They're beautiful!" Valerie said, admiring them.

"Thanks, mom. Joe sent them to my P O Box yesterday. He said they were his apology gift since he reneged on our last three outings together. He claimed he has something else for my birthday."

"Oh...sounds exciting," Valerie responded, trying to hide her irritation.

"It's okay, mom. You don't have to hide how you feel about Joe to spare my feelings. Joe has proven to me on countless occasions that he's not a man of his word. I'm not that little girl crying and holding her teddy bear anymore."

"I know, sweetheart, but he's still your dad." Valerie paused, placing her hand on Dawn's ears. "I know you don't intend for us to get your friends these bling bling diamonds." Valerie joked, lightning the mood.

Dawn laughed. "Of course not, mom. I was thinking something simple. But no clip ons."

They both laughed and walked out of the door. Dawn and her mother actually enjoyed spending time together despite their slightly complicated lives. Her mother didn't invite anyone else into their world in fear of Dawn being exposed.

Dawn was just as cautious as her mom, so she didn't ask to have sleepovers or go to any. As a matter of fact, this was the first social gathering they had ever thrown. And since Dawn had super strength, they didn't need a man around the house for much. Moving was also a breeze since Dawn could carry half the house in one trip without a twitch. Their existence was a unique predicament, but they made it work.

Still fifteen miles outside of town, Valerie stopped at a red-light noticing traffic seem to be at a halt. Dawn peeked her head out the window to see if she could see anything, but the traffic was too heavy. The light had turned green and back red a few times, but nothing was moving.

"Help! Someone help!" A faint voice cried out.
Dawn looked at her mom who already knew what she was thinking.

"Dawn, I don't think it's a good idea."

"But what if someone really needs our help?"

Although Valerie was honored that she had such a compassionate daughter, she wished at times like this she could be as selfish as her dad. It wasn't that Valerie didn't care about others suffering, she was more concerned with Dawn Lynn's safety. Valerie took a deep breath and placed her hand on Dawn Lynn's hand. She realized her baby was growing up into an amazing young woman. She had to allow Dawn Lynn to make decisions for herself. For what good was a hidden treasure? With a gentle squeeze, she smiled and said, "Let's go."

Chapter 7

Dawn Lynn carefully strolled several yards from where her mom was parked. There were no houses or buildings in site on what seemed like a deserted highway. With the exception of the few cars that had lined up, nothing was visible but trees in the far-off distance. If only her mother had taken the interstate like she suggested, they wouldn't be in this predicament. Sometimes her mom could be too cautious. Besides, she was sixteen. No one was going to recognize her from when she was four.

After walking by the few cars, the agonizing screams became less muffled. She had finally made it to the front of the semi-truck and nothing in life could have prepared her for what she saw. Shear horror spread over Dawn's face as she approached the accident. In front of the semi-truck was an overturned car and a frail woman stuck underneath. It didn't appear as if the truck had been involved in the accident since there wasn't any damage to the truck. She also couldn't see anyone in the driver's seat.

She turned her attention back towards the helpless woman underneath the car. She was very pretty and looked as is she may have been in her early twenties. Her long brunette hair was wildly flowing on the concrete road and she had a bruise on her left cheek, which may or may not have been from the accident.

A short and rather thin man with a gun who also had a bloody injury cascading from his forehead was pacing back and forth. It was obvious that he was the driver and was a nervous wreck. He was yelling at the brunette as if she was able to argue back. She couldn't. She just lied there in agony listening to this maniac insult her. Once he noticed Dawn Lynn watching him, he stopped and turned his aggression toward her.

"What are you looking at?" He screamed, pointing the gun at Dawn. "Go back to your car!"

Putting her arms in a surrendering position, she spoke softly. "Sir, I am a certified nurse. I can help her."

She had to lie since this woman's life was as stake. She couldn't understand why this deranged man was waving a gun at someone who was already minutes away from death. Smoke was emerging from the engine. The sight and smell of the dripping gas intensified the danger. Dawn didn't hear any sirens, so she wasn't sure how far the police were from the location or if they were notified at all. She realized if she didn't talk him down soon, the car could explode and possibly hurt or kill everyone in the area. There was no way Dawn was going to allow that to happen.

"Oh yeah...well...I... I don't know if I want her to live."

"Oh, is this your lovely girlfriend?"

"She's supposed to be my lovely wife."

"Okay…Congratulations. I'm sure the wedding will be beautiful."

"There isn't going to be any wedding, lady. That's how we got in this mess in the first place. This is all her fault."

"Okay. I get it. Let's make a deal."

"What?"

"I want to make a deal with you."

"Listen lady. I'm not interested in making any deal. The deal was for this trash to spend the rest of her life with me and now she's saying no."

"I get how you feel. I'd be upset, too. But I have to admit something to you."

"You don't even know me, lady."

"I don't. But I do know a tragedy like this can easily change a woman's heart."

"You think?" He asked, lowering the gun and looking at the trapped woman.

"Think about it. You're the only one to actually experience this with her. Who else will she have who will understand and console her?"

"Uh...yeah. I guess you could be right." He said, slightly moving over as he allowed Dawn Lynn in closer.

"If you allow me to help her, I have a friend who is a marriage counselor and will help you two get back on track."

"We don't have the money for that."

"That's part of the deal. If you allow me to help, I will pay for the session. She'll give me a discount for the referral and also because she has known me eight years."

"You look a little young to have been working eight years."

"No, I mean I've known her since we were in high school."

"Oh, okay," he hesitantly replied, motioning with the gun for her to step in and help.

Even though Dawn wasn't afraid of this man, she didn't trust his actions. He was obviously unpredictable and the sniffling and rubbing of his nose led her to the impression he was on drugs. Dawn couldn't watch her back and save the woman at the same time, so she had to make a dramatic decision.

Feeling the heat of the exposed engine, she put herself in a position where it looked as if she was about to bend over and help the woman. The guy turned his head and had the nerve to attempt to light a cigarette. With a swift move, Dawn Lynn used her super strength and kicked him thirty yards left to a grassy area. It wasn't her intentions to hurt him as she watched him glide through the air, but she needed him out of the way. She didn't see him moving in the distance once he landed, but she didn't have time to check his well-being. Using her spectacular muscles, she bent down, using one hand to lift the car and the other to pull the woman from underneath the wreck. She needed to remove the car out of harms way. She figured throwing it would bring too much attention and she didn't know how damaging the impact would be.

Making sure no other vehicles were coming from the opposite side of the highway, she then took both hands and quickly pushed the car out of harms way. By the time she had made it back to the scene, there was a massive explosion behind her creating a ball of fire that extended towards the sky.

"Dawn, get in! We have to go!" Valerie yelled from the driver's seat.

"But what about the police-"

"They're on the way. We must leave. Now!"

Dawn Lynn hopped over the car and jumped in the passenger seat. She had used her strength before, but never in this capacity. She felt rejuvenated as the blood in her body gave her a warming sensation. She hadn't even noticed her mother driving at full speed until Valerie pulled up in the driveway.

Dawn Lynn didn't have to assume what would happen next. She helped her mother gather their things and put them on the trailer they kept outback under the shed. With the exception of the bedroom sets, living room furniture, and a few televisions, all the other big appliances were rented. Moving had become routine, so it didn't take long.

Although Dawn respected her mother, she'd never felt so alive after doing what she had just did. She decided she wasn't going to stop. Whenever her mother wasn't around, and she saw someone in need, she was going to use her strength to help. And when she turned eighteen, she would go out at night with a disguise. She felt she was doing a good service by helping others. This had to have been the purpose of her journey and if she was doing something good for others, what was the worse that could happen?

Chapter 8

Dawn Lynn fastened the straps to her boxing gloves and pumped her fists together before bringing them up to her face, taking her stance. With quick, succinct strokes, she hit the punching bag in front of her, her toned arms fully engaged. Her father had tried calling again. She let it ring to voicemail. She'd given him enough chances. And after her mother told her about what he was doing with his assistant the day Dawn Lynn almost died... Dawn punched the bag harder this time, a growl of frustration escaping her throat.

Even though she and her dad had the talk about how he loved her no matter what her mom and he went through, it didn't seem to matter. His selfishness had undercut any logical explanation he had about love. The fact of the matter was you don't hurt the people you claim to love.

Dawn Lynn couldn't help but to feel frustrated and that her life had sucked. Dr. Welch's treatment had saved her, yes, but the serum had taken an unexpected twist. Her ability to cope in society was strained. She was not allowed to participate in high school sports or any other physical activity. She had to tone down her participation during physical education, aerobics, weight lifting, and any other class that involved using her muscles.

The best years of her life were essentially the worst. Her teenage years were supposed to be one of the most enjoyable times of her life. All she wanted to do was sprint and break down a few doors, when instead she was confined to acting "normal" and "fitting in." She didn't get to go to any high school dances or join any clubs due to her moving around so much. To make matters even worse, Dawn didn't even attend her high school prom. They had to move two days before the event because Dawn Lynn had stopped a car from running over three children on a sidewalk with her bare hands.

Her super strength wasn't the only thing the serum had done to her. She had also developed a more alert mind and her flexibility made it seem as if every joint in her body was double-jointed. She could run off four hours of sleep easily, which meant lonely nights staying up watching Netflix while the rest of the world slept. Besides, it wasn't as if Dawn has someone to chit-chat with. She didn't have any close friends. She wasn't able to develop any long-lasting relationships with peers because they moved to a different location what seemed like every other year.

When Dawn was young, her mother had always told her they were going on an exciting adventure. Dawn would excitedly load her princess backpack and her mother would have a surprise toy waiting in the back seat. It wasn't until she had gotten older when Dawn realized that they would move every time she instinctively used her strength in public like pushing over a tree to help another little girl save a kitten. Much to Dawn's surprise, this was the longest time they stayed in one place since she could remember.

Her mother had temporarily cut off all ties with her father about a year or so after Dawn had undergone Dr. Welch's treatment. Valerie had attempted to set up father and daughter outings where Dawn could still spend time with him, but Joe missed them all. She figured it would be best to allow Dawn to decide their fate once she had gotten older. Dawn wasn't even allowed to tell her own father about her abilities. That was fine with her. Over time, she came to her own conclusion that her dad was a world-class douche and she'd rather not have much to do with him.

After several hard punches, she removed the gloves with her teeth and threw them to the ground. Exercising kept her momentum and it seemed to heighten the sensation when she went out at night to use her strength. She dropped to the floor and began a series of finger pushups. To finish off her routine she did fifty jumping jacks and seventy-five squats followed by five minutes of alternate one-leg jump roping.

Now that she was twenty-two, she knew exactly how to hide her abilities. Instead of getting a gym membership, she saved up her money to set up gym equipment in the unfinished basement of her mother's home. She'd moved out when she was eighteen to an apartment that was off campus, but still near her college for some much-needed independence. She still visited her mom's home in the mornings for her daily workout.

Today, her mom hadn't been up. She normally was in the kitchen preparing breakfast, so it was a little unusual that she was still in bed. Valerie had restarted her catering business since Dawn Lynn was now in college and things seemed to be as normal as they possibly could be. On a few occasions, her mother would work late and sleep in the next morning, so Dawn wasn't too worried.

Dawn jumped to her feet and took several large gulps of water to rehydrate. A light sheen of sweat shone on her forehead; besides that, she was barely winded. She still hadn't told her mother that she went out at night to help people in need in fear of her mom's reaction. Although she felt as if she had everything under control, she knew her mom would think it was too dangerous and risky. But Dawn figured what were the odds of someone still looking for her after all of these years?

Mounting the swerving stairs to the kitchen, Dawn rooted around her mother's fridge for some breakfast. She made a quick protein shake and avocado on toast. It wasn't until she went to sit at the kitchen table that she noticed a notepad laying on the clean surface. A note was written on it in handwriting she didn't recognize. She hated to pry, but her curiosity had overcome her.

What could her mother be doing that she didn't know about? She had to make sure her mother was okay. Perhaps her mom had met a new guy and was reluctant to tell her about it. Glancing over it, her heart picked up the pace and her mouth went dry when she saw her name on the letter.

Dawn Lynn,

We have taken your mother to our secure facility. We advise you not to contact the police in order to secure your mother's safety. If you do not report to us by six this evening, we are not responsible for what will happen to her. Remember to come alone and enter through the white-gated area. We look forward to meeting with you.

Sincerely,

Anonymous

There was no signature or name left, but an address was scrawled on the bottom. She knew her mom would never play a joke like this, so Dawn knew this was real. She couldn't understand why someone would take her mother. Perhaps her dad was upset from all the money that her mom received in the divorce and wanted revenge. She read the note again and tried to figure out a motive.

What is this – a ransom note? We're living comfortably, but we aren't rich by any means. If anything, they should kidnap dad. Why would someone want to kidnap mom? She wondered.

An icy cold fear clutched at Dawn's insides. Unless… unless they knew about her. What if someone saw her while she was out on one of her night prowls and had been watching her every move since?

It was the one rule her mother had ingrained into her mind: *never* tell anyone about her super strength. There were criminals out there who would exploit her if they got the chance. Dawn racked her brain, trying to think of how someone could have figured it out. She only worked out heavily in her mother's basement, where there were no windows. She hardly ever slipped up when it came to revealing her super strength. She wore her wig, heavy make-up, and dressed in black at night. Her super strength gave her the ability to quickly move before someone could capture a picture or video of her.

Dawn was baffled. She wasn't the only night owl around, but she definitely was the quickest. No one could possibly have noticed her unusual routine. Dawn quickly keyed in the address on the note into her GPS. At this point, it didn't matter how they found out – she just needed to rescue her mother.

Chapter 9

The facility was about an hour away. It was a large science lab that supposedly researched cures for life-threatening diseases. It looked more abandon than it did used according to the Google photo.

If they were trying to save lives, why would they threaten the life of her mom?

Anger boiled in Dawn's blood. She wasn't about to give herself away. She would get her mother back. And she would *not* become a lab rat.

Throwing a black shirt and jacket over her sports bra, Dawn grabbed her car keys and backed out of her mother's driveway, adrenaline pounding through her veins.

Before she could show up at the lab, she'd need some supplies.

Driving into the nearest Walmart's parking lot, she exited her car, marching through the sliding doors. She purchased a tactical vest. It wasn't military grade or anything, but she figured if a stray bullet or two whizzed by, she'd have enough protection.

Next, she grabbed a small pair of binoculars and bought a wicked-looking hunting knife. She cursed herself for not having a gun permit. She wouldn't make that mistake in the future. Feeling satisfied with her purchases, she returned to her car and quickly merged onto the interstate, following her GPS's directions.

The lab was large and windowless, as far as Dawn could tell. Much of it looked like a factory plant. To get to the building, she would have to drive through the security gates as instructed. She knew that would be giving herself away and they would know she was there. It would take away the element of surprise.

She circled around and found a nearby parking lot. In the car, she took off her jacket and pulled on the vest while tugging a sweater around it to keep from looking too suspicious. She hid away the hunter's knife inside her jacket and wrapped the binoculars around her neck.

Exiting her car, she snuck around to the back side of the building, where the security looked less structured. Hiding behind thick shrubbery, she pulled out her binoculars and surveyed the area. Two security personnel stood outside the back gate, talking with each other. As she watched through the binoculars, one of the men turned towards the building's back door, using a key card to unlock it. The light above the door flashed green and he disappeared.

Now there was only one security guard.

Dawn was confident she could take him out.

Emerging from the bushes, she strode right up to him. It took him a moment to notice her, but when he did, he gripped the gun at his belt. "Can I help you, miss?" he asked.

Without a word, Dawn instantly punched him in the jaw, effectively knocking him out. He didn't see it coming. She dragged his body behind a garbage bin and pulled out his keycard and removed his gun and taser from his utility belt. She figured that she may need them later.

Her heart hammering in her ears, she slid the key card in the slot and the door lit green, granting her access. She pulled open the door and stepped through, facing an empty hallway. Dawn was running off pure adrenaline. Step one of her mission was complete.

She roamed the hall, feeling impossibly lost. She doubted there was a map or floor plan to help her out. The building had to be at least three stories tall, and who knew how many stories were underneath?

She needed answers. And she needed them fast.

She turned down a corner and nearly ran into two security guards. Before they could react, she smashed one's head into the wall, cracking it. Noticing the other guard about to react, she quickly wrapped a strong arm around his throat, pinning him against her. He tried to struggle, but she held him fast, crushing his windpipe.

"I *will* kill you," she threatened. "Tell me where my mother is."

She loosened her grip just enough, so the guard could choke out, "I don't know what you're talking about! Is she a patient?"

"Her name is Valerie," Dawn spat. "Valerie Lynn."

He shook his head. "Look, I just patrol the perimeter. I don't know any of the patient's names."

She grit her teeth in frustration.

"Do you know who would know?" she asked, not ready to let him go yet.

"I... I don't know. Ask a doctor, maybe."

"Not helpful."

Dawn bashed his head into the wall to knock him out. He crumpled on top of the other guard. They were out, but they wouldn't be for long. She figured that she had about a half of an hour, tops, to find her mom.

She continued through the building, peering into every room. This floor appeared relatively empty. She wondered if there really were patients here. She wondered where they were keeping them.

Finally, she found the security room. Peeking her head inside, she found two more security guards playing a round of poker, not paying any attention to the camera feed. *Not much must happen around here*, Dawn thought.

She strode into the room, and both guards looked up in surprise. She grabbed them both behind the neck and cracked their skulls together. They slumped on the table, chips flying everywhere, and she scanned the security feed, squinting to find her mother. There were so many rooms, so much to look at. Then, she spotted her.

Her mother was chained to a chair and sitting in front of a table, as if she were being questioned for some violent crime.

Valerie's hair was a matted mess and one eye was bruising – signs of a fight.

Dawn's anger flared. She had reached her breaking point. The tears that almost formed retreated as her blood began to boil. The bastards would pay for doing this to her mother.

She glanced at the camera name. **Basement floor, room 110**

Armed with the information, Dawn left the room, kicking aside discarded cards that stuck in the wall as if they were knives. She found the stairs and quickly descended them, poised to attack anyone who might run into her.

She reached the basement, and slid the keycard through the door, opening it. The hall was barely lit with a few yellow lights overhead. Dawn's body was taut, ready for anything. But again, the hall seemed empty.

Little alarm bells rang in her head that this may be too easy. She pushed her thoughts away. She didn't have time to second-guess herself. She hadn't rescued her mother yet. She walked down the hall until she found room 110. Unlocking it with her keycard, she pushed the door open.

Her mom's head lifted at the noise and her eyes widened when she saw Dawn. "What are you doing here?" she hissed.

"I came to get you, Mom," Dawn said, rushing to her mother's side.

"They know what you can do," Valerie said quickly. "They used me to lure you here…"

The door opened behind Dawn and she whirled as three men spilled into the room. One man who looked to be in his fifties was in a white lab coat with a smug smile on his face. The other two were heavily armed security guards.

"Welcome, Dawn Lynn," the doctor said, shoving his hands in his lab pockets. "Glad you accepted the invitation."

Dawn narrowed her eyes at the doctor. "You knew I was here, didn't you?"

He smiled slowly. "Not only that, I lightened security in the most obvious areas. You may be strong, but you aren't the brightest."

Dawn scowled at him.

"I'm sorry, I've yet to introduce myself," he continued. "My name is Dr. Kline. Dawn, I know that you have a special gift…"

"I don't care who you are," Dawn growled. "Let my mother go!"

Dr. Kline shook his head. "Hear me out first, Miss Lynn."

With a cry, Dawn rushed at him.

One of the guards tased her, and she shuddered, the electricity paralyzing her body and bringing her to her knees.

"No!" her mother screamed. "Please! Don't hurt her!"

Chapter 10

The taser stopped and Dawn held her stomach, waiting for the pain to subside. Dr. Kline's shoes appeared in her vision. She waited for him to speak.

"Dawn, what we require of you is simple, really," he said. "We only need a sample of your blood and your mother can be on her merry way."

Dawn looked up at him. Her eyes were fierce. "But you're implying that I must stay."

He shrugged his shoulders. "Only for a little while. We may need to use you for further testing."

"I'll never let that happen," her mother snapped. "Don't you touch my baby girl."

"How did you know?" Dawn whispered, staring into the doctor's too-blue eyes.

"Quite simple, really," Dr. Kline said. "Do you know the name Greg Mills?"

Dawn shook her head, but she heard her mother suck in a sharp breath. "Dr. Welch's assistant."

"That's right," Dr. Kline said with a smile. "He came to us with all of Dr. Welch's research on you, Dawn, and I have to say – we were quite impressed. Now granted it took years to finally find you, but by sheer coincidence you came to our town."

"I still don't understand how you were able to find me."

"Well, quite frankly, I don't know of too many people being capable of pulling a bus from the ledge of a bridge with their bare hands. I had my guys check into it and wait it out for a while to confirm who you were. I thought it was remarkable and quite frankly too good to be true. You are essential for our study of the human body. Your blood could cure diseases, save lives. Maybe even enhance soldiers."

Dawn shuddered. "I won't let you sell my blood for military use," she said, shakily trying to get to her feet. The guards pointed their guns at her mother.

Dawn's heart leapt inside her throat. They couldn't shoot her – she was too valuable. Her mother, on the other hand…

"Please," Dawn said. "Just let my mother go. I… I'll be your stupid experiment."

Dr. Kline grinned, showing a perfect row of white teeth. "I knew you'd understand," he said gently. He nodded at the guards. "You may take Dawn to her observation cell."

"Dawn, no!" her mother screamed. "You can't do this!"

As the guards approached Dawn, she focused all her energy on what would happen next. As they made to grab her, she drew out her hunting knife, slashing at one guard in the face while power kicking the other. Both guards fell, one out cold, the other went through two walls.

Then, she rounded on Dr. Kline. He took a step back as she slowly walked towards him. Almost tripping over a chair, it was obvious he hadn't armed himself.

"Well, doctor. You may have the muscle, but I guess you aren't the brightest either."

"Listen, Dawn. We can work this out. I'm thinking maybe we can become partners and help others. You do want to help others, don't you?"

His cunning eyes lit in alarm just before she knocked his lights out. He fell against a chair, making a loud noise. It was so much force that the chair stuck in the wall with Dr. Kline in it.

"Shit," Dawn muttered. Someone was bound to have heard that. She easily broke her mother's chains. "Are you alright?" she asked her.

Valerie wrapped her arms around Dawn. "I'm so sorry, baby," she said, holding her tight. "I'm so, so sorry."

"Mom, it's okay," Dawn said, pulling away. "Right now, we have to get out of here."

Her mother nodded, and Dawn led the way out of the room. A few guards were waiting for them outside. Before they could react, Dawn kicked one in the jaw and grabbed another's arm, yanking him so hard he crashed against the wall, smashing his head. Her mother's eyes widened in shock.

Dawn grabbed her mother's hand and led her to the basement stairs. Another guard was coming down them, but she grabbed his arm when he extended it out to tase her and sent him soaring in the air until he crashed into some equipment on the opposite side of the room.

Alarm bells sounded. The security lights flashed white and red as the sirens screamed in their ears. Valerie pressed her hands on either side of her head, squeezing her eyes shut. Dawn grabbed her mother by the hand. They couldn't give up that easily.

Together, they ran up the steps, where several guards ran around in confusion. Anyone who got too close was smashed to the ground or chucked across the hall. Dawn couldn't help laughing. She had never unleashed like this before. It felt so powerful, so *easy.*

Finally, they reached the back exit and Dawn punched her fist right through the door, smashing it off its hinges. She picked up the door as other guards flocked around her. Making sure her mother was securely behind her, she swung the metal door around, knocking guards off their feet and using it as a shield as they sprayed them with bullets.

"No! You can't kill her!" yelled one of the guards. "Doctor Kline will kill us!"

Although the bullets had ceased, it took another ten minutes to knock out several guards that attempted to apprehend her.

Her mom gaped at the fallen men.

"There's no time to gawk, Mom," Dawn said.

They ran to Dawn's car and she spun out of the parking lot, taking the interstate in the opposite direction of home.

They might be runaways now, but at least her mom was safe. It didn't take being a rocket scientist to realize they probably wouldn't be able to return home. They would have to move even further away and start all over again. Lucky for Dawn, she was accustomed to the routine. With her mom back at her side, she was back to being unstoppable.

Thank you for your purchase! Here are some additional books by the author.

Get More Books

Guides

Unleashing Essential Oils: With Extra Invaluable Beauty Tips

E-book Supplier for First Time Home Buyer

My Diet Your Diet Our Diet

Experience of Life vs. Expert Advice

Children Book

Little Cupcake's First Day

Novels and Novellas

Partially Broken Never Destroyed I, II, III, IV, V, VI

Alyce Leaves Wonderland

Coming Soon

A Crime for Two

www.ingramcontent.com/pod-product-compliance
Lightning Source LLC
Chambersburg PA
CBHW022054170626
46808CB00003B/1464